Hobby Horses,

Silly Gooses and Other

Invented Guests

By

Kay Gingrich

Illustrated by Alice Ann Strausbaugh

Hobby Horses, Silly Gooses and Other Invited Guests
by Kay Gingrich
Illustrated by Alice Ann Strausbaugh

Printed in the United States of America

ISBN 9781619047037

www.xulonpress.com

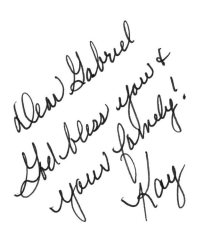

Dear Gabriel
God bless you &
your family!
Kay

It was Christmas Eve in the
Wickersham house. The wee
Wickershams were asleep.
The fire in the fireplace
shed it's warm glow,
and the snow outside
grew deep.

What a glorious tree
it was this year.
It was better than years
before. Lights
twinkled
and dazzled.
There was tinsel
and beads and
popcorn strings
and much more.

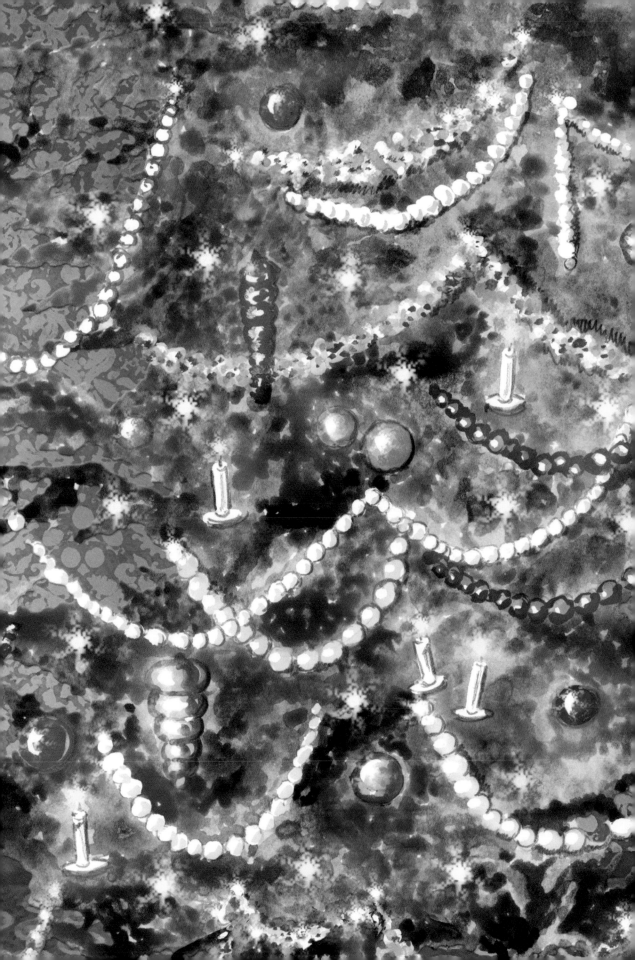

As the old clock
struck twelve, a
sound could be heard.
It was under the tree,
so it seemed.
There drawing close
was a magnificent
sight, one only
imagined or
dreamed.

A scurry
was heard,
tiny feet moved
quickly.
What was that I saw...
was that the doll,
Miss Pick Me?

Surely she wasn't
having a party
without inviting
some friends?
Then, there I saw it,
a tiny tea table,
with teacups
and flowers
with stems.

Miss Pick Me invited
a most unusual group.
There was Silly and Fuzzy
and Hobby and Scoop.
There was Lilly (the
lampshade) and Bang, the gun.
Why... she had invited
nearly everyone.

Miss Music Box played and
played and twirled, and offered
the best of the musical world.
Hobby Horse rocked
to the music that night.
Fuzzy Bear rolled on
the floor with delight!

Scoop the ice cream tender
filled Lilly the Lampshade
with an ice cream called Splendor.
With the party near over
and no chimes to be rung,
well old Bang pulled a good one
and popped his gun.

They all ran
for cover and
into their spots.
But what about Silly?

**Did you think
I forgot?**

Let's see now. Who came
to Miss Pick Me's party?
There was Lilly, Music Box,
Bang, and Scoop and Arty?

There was Fuzzy,
no Arty, but there
was Hobby Horse.
There was you...
YES, YOU...

Silly Goose
of course!!!

CPSIA information can be obtained
at www.ICGtesting.com
Printed in the USA
260538LV00002B